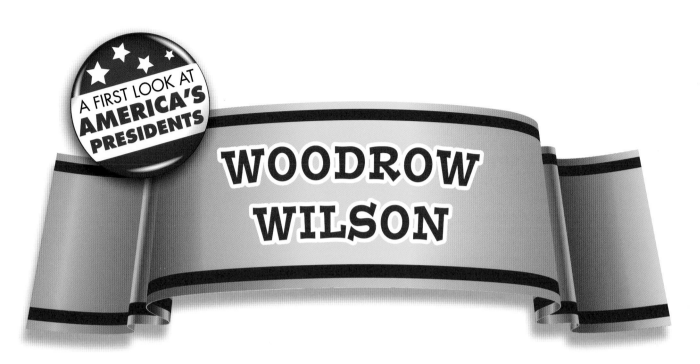

A FIRST LOOK AT AMERICA'S PRESIDENTS

WOODROW WILSON

The 28th President

by Miriam Aronin

Consultant: David Greenberg
Professor of History
Rutgers University
New Brunswick, New Jersey

BEARPORT
PUBLISHING

New York, New York

Credits

Cover, Courtesy White House Historical Association (White House Collection); 4, Courtesy Library of Congress; 5, Courtesy White House Historical Association (White House Collection); 7T, © Everett Historical/Shutterstock; 7B, Courtesy Woodrow Wilson Presidential Library; 8, Courtesy Library of Congress; 9, © Aoldman/Dreamstime; 9R, Courtesy Woodrow Wilson Presidential Library; 10, Courtesy Utah State Historical Society; 11T, Courtesy Library of Congress; 11B, Courtesy Library of Congress; 12, © Corbis; 13T, © Look and Learn; 13B, © Everett Historical/Shutterstock; 14, © Everett Historical/Shutterstock; 15T, Courtesy Library of Congress; 15B, © Everett Collection/Shutterstock; 16, Courtesy Library of Congress; 17T, Courtesy Woodrow Wilson Presidential Library; 17M, © Smithsonian Image Archives, Image 1981.3024.25; 17B, Courtesy Library of Congress; 18, © Zack Frank/Shutterstock; 19, © Roy Kenyon; 19 Sign, © Quinn Dombrowski; 22, © Ken Wolter/Shutterstock; 24, © Yangchao/Shutterstock.

Publisher: Kenn Goin
Editor: Jessica Rudolph
Creative Director: Spencer Brinker
Production and Picture Research: Shoreline Publishing Group LLC

Library of Congress Cataloging-in-Publication Data

Names: Aronin, Miriam, author.
Title: Woodrow Wilson : the 28th president / by Miriam Aronin.
Description: New York, New York : Bearport Publishing, 2016. | Series: A
    first look at America's presidents | Includes bibliographical references
    and index. | Audience: 4–8.
Identifiers: LCCN 2015040017| ISBN 9781943553303 (library binding) | ISBN
    1943553300 (library binding)
Subjects: LCSH: Wilson, Woodrow, 1856–1924—Juvenile literature. |
    Presidents—United States—Biography—Juvenile literature. | United
    States—Politics and government,—1913–1921—Juvenile literature.
Classification: LCC E767 .A665 2016 | DDC 973.913092—dc23
LC record available at http://lccn.loc.gov/2015040017

For more information, write to Bearport Publishing Company, Inc., 45 West 21st Street, Suite 3B, New York, New York 10010. Printed in the United States of America.

10 9 8 7 6 5 4 3 2

CONTENTS

A Better World

Woodrow Wilson had big ideas. He believed in fair treatment for workers. He wanted nations to work together. In many ways, Wilson worked hard to make the world better.

Wilson wanted all people, such as these factory workers, to have safer working conditions.

Wilson's full name is Thomas Woodrow Wilson. As a child, he was called Tommy. As an adult, he was called Woodrow.

Woodrow Wilson was the 28th president of the United States. He served from 1913 to 1921.

Growing Up

Tommy was born in 1856. He grew up mainly in Georgia. Tommy worked hard in school. After school, he loved playing baseball. He became a leader on his baseball team.

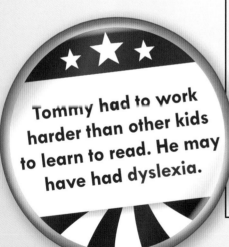

Tommy had to work harder than other kids to learn to read. He may have had dyslexia.

The red letters show what some people with dyslexia might see when they try to read.

Tommy's childhood home

Wilson loved baseball his whole life. As president, he threw a ball at the World Series.

College Life

Woodrow Wilson loved learning. He did well in college. After school, he became a college professor. He taught history and politics. He also wrote books about these subjects. He even ran for political office.

Wilson married Ellen Axson (standing) in 1885. They had three daughters—Jessie, Margaret, and Eleanor.

Wilson was a professor at Princeton University. He was a very popular teacher. He became president of the school in 1902.

Princeton University is located in New Jersey.

Helping Workers

In 1910, Wilson ran for governor of New Jersey and won. Two years later, he ran for president of the United States. People liked Wilson's ideas and voted him into office. As president, he helped workers. He even worked to end **child labor**.

Railroad workers had to work very long hours. Wilson helped make their workdays shorter.

Children workers in a cloth factory

While he was president, Wilson's wife, Ellen, died. He married his second wife, Edith Galt, in 1915.

Edith

11

Attack!

In 1914, World War I began in Europe. German **submarines** started attacking ships in the Atlantic Ocean. Many Americans died in the attacks. Wilson had a tough decision. He wanted to keep Americans safe. Yet he and most Americans did not want to go to war.

Submarines, or subs, can travel above and below the water's surface. They sink ships by shooting underwater missiles at them.

In 1915, a German sub sank a ship called the *Lusitania*. More than 1,000 people died, including 128 Americans.

In World War I, German soldiers (below) fought against British and French soldiers, who were known as the Allies.

America Goes to War

Wilson convinced the Germans to stop attacking ships—for a time. The attacks started again in 1917. Wilson had had enough. He decided to enter the war. The Americans helped the Allies win the war in 1918.

Posters like this one asked men to join the U.S. military.

BE A U.S. MARINE!
307 Evening Star Building, Washington, D. C.

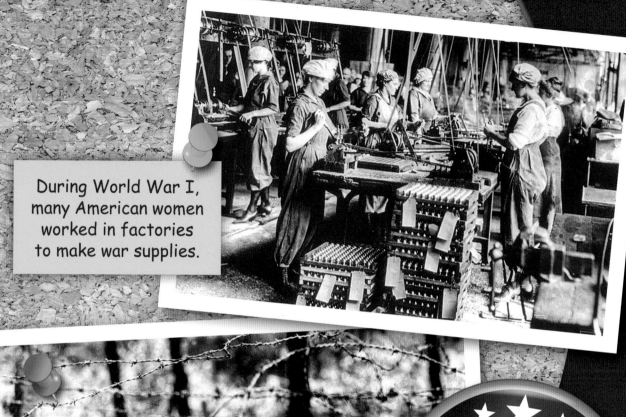

During World War I, many American women worked in factories to make war supplies.

About four million American soldiers took part in the war. More than 300,000 were injured or killed.

15

After the War

When the war ended, Wilson was very busy. He met with leaders in Europe to prevent more wars. He also supported women's rights. In the early 1900s, most women could not vote. In 1920, a new law gave American women this important right.

Wilson (far right) with leaders in Europe after World War I

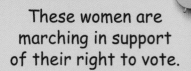
These women are marching in support of their right to vote.

PRESIDENT WILSON SAYS: "This is the time to support Woman Suffrage."

VOTES FOR WOMEN

In 1919, Wilson had a stroke. He was ill for the rest of his time as president. His wife Edith took care of him and helped him with his work.

17

Remembering Wilson

Today, we remember Woodrow Wilson for both his ideas and his actions. Wilson believed in fairness. He supported laws to help workers. He wanted nations to work together for peace. His work helped make the United States a leader in the world.

Many places around the world are named after Wilson. The Wilson Center is in Washington, DC. Experts there look for ways to solve world problems.

This street in Paris, France, is named after Wilson.

16e Arr.t

AVENUE
DU
PRÉSIDENT
WILSON
1856 - 1924
PRÉSIDENT DES ÉTATS-UNIS
D'AMÉRIQUE

19

TIMELINE

Here are some major events from Woodrow Wilson's life.

1856
Thomas Woodrow Wilson is born in Staunton, Virginia.

1860
Wilson's family moves to Augusta, Georgia.

1850   1860   1870   1880

1866
Wilson cannot read until age ten, possibly because he had dyslexia.

1885
Wilson marries Ellen Axson.

1912
Wilson wins the race for president of the United States.

1902
Wilson becomes president of Princeton University.

BE A U.S. MARINE!
307 Evening Star Building, Washington, D. C.

1914
World War I begins in Europe. Ellen Wilson dies.

1920
The Nineteenth Amendment gives women all over the country the right to vote.

| 1890 | 1900 | 1910 | 1920 | 1930 |

1915
Wilson marries Edith Galt.

1918
World War I ends.

1924
Wilson dies in Washington, DC.

21

FACTS and QUOTES

"We cannot be separated in interest or divided in purpose. We stand together until the end."

When Wilson dated Edith Galt, they could not meet very often. So they wrote each other love letters. In one letter, Wilson wrote, "Do you think it is an accident that we found each other at this time?"

Wilson loved the new technology of the early 1900s, such as movies, radios, and cars. He didn't know how to drive, but a driver took him on a car ride every day when he was president.

"What we demand in this war . . . is that the world be made fit and safe to live in; and particularly that it be made safe for every peace-loving nation."

WOODROW WILSON
1856–1924

GLOSSARY

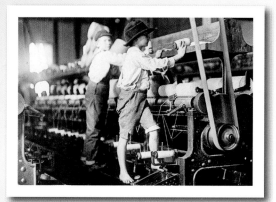

child labor (CHILD LAY-bur) when young children work at jobs, often for long hours in unsafe conditions

dyslexia (diss-LEK-see-uh) difficulty in reading because a person may see letters or words in the wrong order

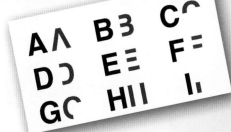

stroke (STROHK) the breaking or blocking of a blood vessel in the brain that causes the loss of feeling, movement, or thought

submarines (SUHB-muh-reenz) ships that can travel under the water as well as on the water's surface

Index

Read More

Frith, Margaret. *Who Was Woodrow Wilson?* New York: Grosset & Dunlap (2015).

Waxman, Laura Hamilton. *Woodrow Wilson (History Maker Bios).* Minneapolis, MN: Lerner (2006).

Learn More Online

To learn more about Woodrow Wilson, visit
www.bearportpublishing.com/AmericasPresidents

About the Author:
Miriam Aronin writes and edits books for kids. She lives in Chicago, Illinois.